From the World of

HEADFIRST

Orphan Stories

TIM PELTON

CONTENTS

Boys' Town

It was during the first week of January, 1968, that Jamie decided it was time, once and for all, to lose his virginity.

For years he had been fantasizing about the girl who would finally escort him into that far and fabled land. Sometimes she was a randy redhead whose clothes had buttons that practically undid themselves. At other times, she was a shy blonde who begged him to be gentle as her nightgown slid to the floor. They were tall, short, slender, heavy, black, brown, Asian, with large breasts, small breasts, bushy pubic hair, even shaved bald. He had them standing up, face-to-face, dog-style, head-to-toes in a hammock, in groups, or solo. In age they went from fourteen year-old girls suggestively jumping rope to middle-aged women looking for a quickie in the back room of the super market. Over his teenage years this lusty mob had almost constantly paraded through his imagination. Luckily, he discovered masturbation; otherwise his testicles may have ruptured before he reached sixteen.

In reality, there had been a few opportunities to get laid, but, he would tell himself, things just hadn't worked out. The truth was that he'd gotten terrified and ran. To a teenage boy, few things are more frightening than the prospect of a teenage girl laughing in your face.

After he'd joined the Army, Jamie's frustration only grew. When the guys would hang around the Coke machine and tell stories about their sexual adventures, Jamie, not wanting to admit he'd had none, would make up a few lies and casually toss them out. He had the feeling that some, if not most, of the other stories were even bigger lies than his own, but no one ever bothered to question them. Every now and then he'd find himself, in his bunk after lights out, quietly jacking off into a sock.

So it followed that when Ernie Simms, a half-crazed redneck from Alabama, threw an arm around Jamie's shoulders one night and said, "Me and Johnson and a couple of guys are going down to Juarez this weekend and fuck us a few whores. You interested?" Jamie ignored the little voice in the back of his head that was screaming "No! No!" and said "Hell, yes."

Two days later, Jamie was sitting in the back seat of an old Chevy sedan that was parked in front of a small market in Ciudad Juarez, Mexico. Dillman and Kovadnek, a couple of guys from Jamie's Company, sat in the front seat and tried to look relaxed. Simms, who made the trip across the border frequently, had insisted that they stop for a couple of six packs before heading on to "Boys' Town". "Just to get tuned up," he explained. "It makes the whores better lookin'."

Simms and Johnson came out of the store, each of them carrying a broken six-pack and greedily chugging a beer. They piled into the back seat and passed the cans around.

Jamie nursed his beer and wondered to himself how an odd pair of friends like Simms and Fred Johnson had fallen in together. Where Simms was short and swarthy, Johnson was a tall, pie-faced blonde, a son of a Swedish lumberjacking family from Washington State. About the only thing they had in common was a love of "gettin' drunk and raisin' hell". Jamie supposed that was enough.

Not long afterwards, they had paid a couple of bucks to a toothless old man, parked on a dirt lot next to several other cars with American plates, and walked into "Boys' Town" a section of the city reserved for Prostitution. To Jamie, it was like taking a stroll through Hell. The dirt streets smelled like an open sewer, the walls were urine-stained. Nearly every building was a bar with a man or two out front bellowing the merits of the girls within in Spanish and broken English. Simms was taking them to "the best bar on the street" and to get there they had to step over a passed-out drunk and avoid the growling, mangy dog that was lapping up the man's vomit.

Suddenly a screaming argument tumbled out into the street in front of them. A middle-aged woman and a drunken man were fighting over a wad of money. He was trying to pry the greenbacks out of her hand as she shrieked and swore and scratched his face. She kicked him hard in the balls. He doubled over for a second, then swung a shaky roundhouse punch at her face, missed, and fell sprawling into the dirt.

At that moment, Jamie felt a small, spidery hand grabbing at his crotch. He squeaked and jumped back in shocked surprise. An old, wrinkled woman, dressed in black, sat on a folding chair against the wall. She held her hand out and gestured to him to come back as she giggled obscenely.

Jamie turned and looked wildly for his friends. He finally saw them heading down the street and he ran to catch up.

Five minutes later they were standing in front of The Lone Star Bar and Simms was announcing, "This is the place! Gentlemen, I am ready to get me some pussy!"

Laughing and pounding each other on the back, Simms and Johnson walked in. The other three followed.

Jamie had expected either a raucous strip club with naked dancers, loud drunks and free-flowing tequila, or a gaudy sitting room with semi-dressed women who draped themselves on the furniture in fetching poses and hoped to be chosen. Instead, there were about a dozen tables and an empty dance floor. Around the periphery were a bar, a jukebox, and some benches against the walls. On these benches sat twelve or fifteen women. The women wore cheap, too-tight cocktail dresses and heavy makeup. They smoked cigarettes and talked among themselves.

The five soldiers sat around one of the tables and ordered beers from an aged waiter who nodded and shuffled off to the bar. Some of the women from the benches got up and sauntered over to the table.

Simms turned to the first one that got there and smiled broadly. "Hey there, honey. What's your name?"

"Maria," the woman said as she slid into an empty chair next to Simms, who turned and leered proudly to the rest of the table as if he'd just picked up the prettiest girl at the dance.

Johnson grabbed the arm of a woman who was taller, heavier, and homelier than Maria and steered her into a chair next to him.

"You're in good hands, baby," Fred laughed, "My name's Freddy and I'm ready!"

Within a short time there were women all around the table, one for every guy – except Jamie. Even dorky Dillman was sitting next to a woman with crooked teeth and a mustache who was steaming up his glasses. But Jamie sat by himself, sipping his beer and trying to look nonchalant, quietly wondering what the hell those other prostitutes were waiting for.

The first thing each of the women did was to request a drink. The old waiter returned with a glass of heavily diluted wine and the soldier paid the inflated price. Then the bargaining began.

Simms had previously told them that the going price was eight to ten dollars.

"The whores'll ask for twenty," he counseled, "You offer five, they'll come back at fifteen and so on. That's just a straight fuck, anything extra..."

"A dog fuck and a blow job?" Johnson yelled.

"Yeah, all that, they'll want more for that shit. And don't take any money bigger than a five, ain't nobody gonna give you change down there."

Jamie sat there uncomfortably, trying to decipher the small print in Spanish on his beer bottle's label while all around him the negotiations went forward.

It is difficult not to stare when the fellow sitting next to you has a woman muttering in his ear while her hand is squeezing the bulge in his jeans. So Jamie looked around the bar. He noticed at least four or five prostitutes sitting on the benches against the wall, smoking their cigarettes and talking. It seemed to him that they were trying to avoid eye contact whenever he looked their way.

Simms stood up. Ever the Southern gentleman, Simms pulled the chair out for his "date" and as she rose he grinned wickedly at the rest of the table.

"Gentlemen" he said, and followed the woman out a door in the back of the bar. Johnson and his whore quickly followed, then the others. Jamie found himself alone at the table with nothing for company but a few empty beer bottles.

It wasn't like he'd never felt rejection before. Remembering being turned down by Robin Ann Murbaugh when Jamie asked her to the Junior Prom still made him wince. But these were whores in a dilapidated

Mexican bar who were ignoring him. Rather than hang around feeling like a big turd, he decided to just go back to the car and wait for the others.

Jamie stood up, and then told himself he hadn't come down to Juarez to sit in the back seat of Dillman's car in a dusty parking lot. He looked around and noticed a woman sitting by herself against the wall on the other side of the bar. She was a little older and more shop-worn than the others, but at this point, Jamie didn't really care. He walked over to her.

She looked up at him with dead eyes and said, "Hey Joe, you wanna party? I fuck you real good for twenty dollah."

"I don't know," Jamie answered, "Don't you think that's a little excessive"

"Huh?"

"It's too much."

"You wan' half an' half?"

"No, just a straight fuck. I'll give you eight dollars."

She gave him an expression like he'd just offered her a dead rat covered with moldy cheese.

"Eight dollah. Hmmph. All right, all right," she grumbled as she got up. "Come on, Cheapyskate. Let's go.

In a moment they were walking through the same small back door through which all of his friends had disappeared.

Jamie stepped outside and stopped for a moment to let his eyes adjust to the semi-darkness.

A single, naked light bulb high above the back door provided the only outside illumination for a long, narrow row of shacks jammed together shoulder-to-shoulder behind the bar. Each shack had several doors fronting onto a wooden walkway.

Jamie followed the woman down the walk. She stopped at one of the doors, unlocked it, and led Jamie in. The room was very small, big enough only for a double bed, a chest of drawers, a dressing table, and barely enough space to walk between.

She ordered Jamie to take off his clothes and sit on the bed. He complied, dropping the clothing in a pile against the wall. As he sat on the bed, his feet sticking out in front of him, he looked down at his penis nestled coyly in his lap. He wished he could will it to do a good job and not embarrass him, but he knew all he could do was thrust and hope. The damned thing would do what it would do and ignore his wishes completely. He was just the bag of meat and bones attached to its back end.

The prostitute had, by then, removed all of her clothing except panties and brassiere. She was lighting small votive candles in front of two pictures on the dressing table, one picture of the Virgin Mary and the other of some other female saint. She got down on her knees, bowed her head to pray, crossed herself, stood up, and stripped off her panties.

"For eight dollah, I don' take off no bra" she announced, then climbed onto the bed.

After a good look at her sagging, lumpy flesh, Jamie felt that the bra staying on was probably a blessing.

She grabbed his penis and began jerking on it rhythmically. Her hand was rough and dry and the experience was more painful than exciting. He closed his eyes, mentally substituting one of his stable of fantasy girls, and soon he had an erection. Not a whopping hard-on, but stiff enough to cause the whore to roll over on her back and pull him on top.

She quickly stuffed him into her vagina, threw her legs over his and said, "Okay, Joe. Let's go."

He was inside her! He was sliding his dick back and forth inside a living woman. This was the moment he'd been thinking/fantasizing/lying about and waiting for years. He concentrated on the feeling so later he could remember it clearly. Suddenly he realized he was coming. Six strokes in and he was coming! Quick, think of something else! Windshield wipers on a rainy night – galoshes with buckles – Oh shit! Oh shit!

Feeling the hot liquid inside her, the whore asked, "You finish? You finish?" and tried to push him off.

"No. Not yet," Jamie muttered grimly as he kept thrusting away. His penis was quickly losing size and stiffness. A few moments later the flaccid thing fell out of her and he was clearly done.

"Okay, you finish. Get off," The prostitute ordered as she pushed him away.

She stepped off the bed, grabbed a tissue out of a box on the dresser, and dropped it into Jamie's lap. Then she stooped down and pulled a large, galvanized steel washtub out from under the bed. A sponge floated in three inches of water that slopped against the sides of the tub. She squatted over the tub and, using the sponge, began to vigorously douche herself.

Watching this actually lifted some of the depression that had fallen on him. Here was another soul hoping for some kind of control over bodily functions that were relentlessly unmanageable. All she had to protect herself against pregnancy and venereal disease was a tub of water and the Virgin Mary.

Jamie dressed himself, fished eight dollars out of his wallet, and dropped them on the dressing table. The whore was now sitting on the bed, smoking a cigarette, and ignoring him as she picked at something on her leg. He headed for the door, giving the washtub a wide berth. She obviously didn't change the water between clients and he didn't even want to think about, let alone see, what might be floating around in there.

* * *

Jamie walked through the small door back into the main building and saw the heavy-set Kovadnek leaning on the bar and drinking a beer.

"Corporal K," Jamie said as he put an elbow on the bar, "How'd it go? Where is everybody?"

"It went, I guess," Kovadnek answered, "Better'n fuckin' my fist, I suppose. Johnson heard a rumor that there's a stage show at one of these joints and the gal is doing a Donkey Act. He and Simms had a couple shots of Tequila and then went off to find it."

"What's a Donkey Act?"

"The gal leads a donkey out on stage, somehow gets the donkey hard, and fucks him."

"You're shitting me."

"Not you, man," Kovadnek grinned, "You're my favorite turd. Anyway, I'm just saying what Johnson told me. He was all excited."

"Yeah, I'll bet," Jamie said, " I'm kinda hungry. Want to go see if we can scare up some chow?"

"Hey, good idea," Kovdnek patted his ample stomach, "Lead on, man"

Jamie and Kovadnek stepped out the front door. Across the street and several bars to the left, Jamie saw a "Restaurante" sign.

"How about down there?"

"Sure. What the hell. As long as we're going to get the clap we may as well have a little ptomaine to go with it."

They stepped off the curb, waited for a drunken Mariachi band to pass, and then crossed to the other side of the street.

"Oh, hey," Jamie said, "What happened to Dillman, he go with Johnson and Simms?"

"Nah," came the reply, "He's still in there with that gal."

"Really? Dillman? "

"Yeah, the little twerp," Kovadnek shrugged, "he told me once he could go on humping away just about as long as he wanted. I figured he was yankin' my chain."

Jamie didn't say anything more for a while. Now as well as humiliation and embarrassment, he had to deal with jealousy.

* * *

Not long after, Jamie was working on the last few bites from a plate of enchiladas and thinking about wringing Dillman's neck when the Pfc in question came through the door.

"There you guys are!" Dillman yelled in a high, excited voice, "I've been looking all over for you. She stole it from me and you gotta come help me get it back."

"Stole what?" Jamie asked, all wide-eyed innocence, "your dick?"

"No, dipshit, my wallet. If all three of us go over there, we might be able to get it back."

Jamie looked over at Kovadnek. They both shrugged and stood up. Personally, they may have considered Dillman to be something of a dink, but right now he was an American GI from their Company and he needed help.

On the way back to the Lone Star, Dillman told them the story. After he had finished, the whore had picked up his clothes and handed them to him, barely letting him get dressed before she shoved him out the door. That was when he discovered his wallet was missing. He had tried to get back in, but the door was locked.

"I figure with three of us out there threatening to kick the door in, she might give it back."

As they walked through the bar Jamie considered this plan. He was having his doubts as they came out through the little door and into the semi-darkness surrounding the rear shacks.

Dillman went ahead trying to figure out which of the many doors was the one he had come out of.

Kovadnek turned to Jamie and muttered, "What if they got guys back here to, y'know, kick the shit out of any John who starts raisin' hell with the whores?"

Dillman had found the right door and started banging on it.

"Open up in there!" he yelled, "Gimme back my wallet!"

"Go 'way," came the muffled reply, "You take too long."

"Open up, goddamn it or we'll kick the door in!"

"Fuck you!"

Dillman signaled to Jamie and Kovadnek. Jamie moved carefully up the walk, peering into the shadows expecting at any time to see goons with clubs come stepping out. Then up ahead he saw some movement low to the ground and heard a rumbling animal growl.

"What's that?" he whispered, "A dog? They've got a dog? Oh man, we're fucked."

Jamie was wondering which would be the best way to run when out of the darkness came the sounds of retching and then of vomit splashing in the dirt.

He heard a familiar southern accent moan, "Jeezis Fuckin' Christ."

Jamie relaxed.

"Hey, Simms. Is that you?"

What he had thought to be a dog ready to attack was Ernie Simms on his hands and knees. Simms sat up and turned to look. Then he grinned drunkenly. A prostitute stood next to him, arms folded, with a disgusted look on her face.

"Gentlemen," Simms said as he pulled himself to his feet using different parts of the whore as handholds, "I'm thinkin' I'm gonna have me one last go around."

Simms brushed the mud off his knees and, with concentration, was able to step up onto the wooden walkway. By the time he had done so, the whore had already unlocked one of the doors and gone inside.

"All right then," Jamie grinned, "Carry on Mr. Simms."

Simms returned Jamie's salute left-handed, and headed for the open door.

"Hey Simms!" someone bellowed from farther up the walkway.

Simms stopped and turned.

"Hey Johnson!" Simms yelled back, "Did you get any on ya?"

Some drunks, like Simms, move slowly and unsteadily as if they're ninety years old and afraid they might fall and break a hip. Johnson, on the other hand, was the opposite way. With every shot of Tequila his stride seemed to lengthen. Right now the big Swede was positively loping.

"Nah," he yelled in answer to Simms' question, "I was too drunk, man. I couldn't get it up. Hey, how about letting me watch you?"

"Not only No, but Fuck No"

"C'mon Simms, it'll be fun!"

"Get away from me, you twisted fuck. You want a thrill, go buttfuck the bartender."

And with that, Simms walked into the room and the door slammed shut in Johnson's face. Johnson stared at the closed door for a moment, then doubled up a ham-sized fist and began to pound on it.

"C'mon Simms!" he bawled, "Lemme in! You won't even know I'm there!"

With every blow of Johnson's fist, the door shook in its frame.

"I won't even look at your wrinkled Alabama ass bobbin' up and down, I promise!"

Suddenly the door jerked open and Simms' whore appeared in the doorway in her bra and panties. In her hands was the galvanized washtub. Too surprised to move, Johnson just stood there as she threw the contents in his face.

* * *

Later on, on the way back to Fort Hood, a soaked and stinking Johnson sat by himself in the rear of Dillman's car. All the windows were open. Jamie and the other three, crammed into the front seat, tried to ignore the bleats of innocence and indignation coming from behind them.

DENVER POP

Jamie was once more standing in a line to enter a stadium but the differences far outweighed the similarities. This time he was not waiting to get in to see Lisa run in the Colorado Small College State track meet, this time she was standing next to him. And he was not standing in a single line to buy a ticket, he was in one of twenty lines and he already held two tickets in his hand. The tickets read "Denver Pop Festival, Saturday, June 28th 1969, Mile High Stadium, Denver"

Jamie put his arm around Lisa's shoulders. She leaned into him and kissed his cheek. Then, laughing, she quickly stepped out of his grasp to move forward with the line. She turned to give him a playful look that said, "Well, come on" and he stepped up next to her and once more held her against his side.

She's being very affectionate today, he said to himself. *After that fight last night I was afraid that today was gonna be icebox city.*

But now here they were, tighter than ever, getting ready for five or six hours of the best rock 'n' roll in the world. And Jamie was starting to get off on that tab of White Cloud he'd dropped just before they got out of the car. He smiled.

This is gonna be so far out.

One of the ticket outlets for the festival was the music store in Colton where Harvey worked and Harvey had held back several blocks of tickets for his friends.

While they were in line, Lisa had noticed Waltz, Jill, McNulty and Krenovich in the next line and about 20 people back. So after going through the turnstiles and having their tickets torn in half, Lisa suggested that Jamie wait for them while she took her stub and went up to locate seats. Jamie's brain had, due to the onset of the drug, begun to take the scenic route on its way to making decisions. By the time he'd come to the conclusion that he should be the one to go, Lisa had disappeared and his friends were coming up to him and waving.

Jamie smiled to see that all of them had dilated eyes, flushed cheeks, and that jumpy as a deer-in-the-headlights look.

"Do you like my new house?" Jamie gestured around him, "I may have invited a few too many people to the house-warming, whattya think?"

"Weak, my man, pretty weak," said Krenovich, "Hey there's a guy selling programs, anybody want a program?"

"Seriously, Dude," asked McNulty, "You can read? Or did you not get off yet? What does that sign say?"

He pointed to a sign over their heads. Jamie could make out the word "Attention", but all the letters in the body of the text were doing the Cha-cha with one another. He quickly gave up trying to make them out.

Krenovich squinted hard and finally said, slowly, as if he were sounding out the words, "If you light up a joint, please remember to share a toke with the ushers."

"Liar" Jill rolled her eyes. Everybody laughed.

"Lisa went ahead to find the seats," Jamie said, "Come on, I think she went up that ramp."

Although the ramp was fairly crowded, people were moving steadily along. When they got about halfway up, Jamie thought he heard someone yelling and looked up ahead. There was Lisa at the top of the ramp. She had climbed halfway up on the railing and she was pointing back down the ramp directly at him. And she was shouting at the top of her lungs.

"Look, everybody, look! It's Keith Moon! The drummer for the Who! Look! Keith Moon!"

To his horror, Jamie watched several hundred people stop, turn around, and stare at him. Jamie covered his face with his hands and scuttled up the ramp, blushing like a crimson Christmas tree bulb. When he got to Lisa she was so weak with laughter she had to cling to the railing to keep from falling down.

"Hiya ha hahaha," she chortled, "I knew you were gonna be mad, but you know what? It was worth it! God, the look on your face. Hee heeheehee."

Jamie tried to work up some anger, but Lisa, laughing, was completely enchanting. Little sparkles seemed to dance in the air around her, enticing you to laugh along.

"Okay, okay, you had your big laugh," Jamie said. "Now which way to our seats?"

"Over there somewhere," she gestured vaguely to the right while smothering a giggle, "Come on, let's go find 'em"

Their seats turned out to be pretty good, all-in-all, only a little way off to one side, and several rows back from an aisle. Waltz and Jill were on their left while McNulty and Krenovich had the seats to their right.

A band had been playing as they came in, and they were announcing the last song of their set. The tune began with a fuzzy guitar riff against a tinkley organ.

"Who is this?" Jamie asked McNulty. "The Strawberry Alarm Clock?"

"Sounds like 'em, doesn't it?" McNulty made a sour face as he bit down on the filter of his cigarette with his front teeth, "I think they're called Aorta, at least that's what it says on the bass drum."

A joint rolled in yellow paper that had been making its way down the row got to Jamie. He took a toke and passed it to Lisa, who passed it to Jill. Jamie watched the joint move down the row and noticed a twelve year-old boy making his way up the other way. On his round face he wore round glasses and a serious expression. He was clutching a program and excusing himself to the people as he stepped on their feet and bumped into their knees.

The band hit the final chord of the song, took their bows, and left the stage while the roadies began breaking taking things apart and making room for the next act to set up.

The boy, still coming, finally stopped in front of Jill and looked at Jamie.

"Sorry to bother you Mr. Moon," the kid said solemnly, "but would you sign my program?"

"Look man, I'm sorry to disappoint you but I'm not..."

Jamie felt Lisa's elbow bounce into his ribs. He glanced at her and saw she was biting her lip in an effort not to laugh out loud. The kid, undeterred, held out a program in one hand and a felt tip pen in the other.

Jamie rolled his eyes and wrote "Jamie Shipman" on the program and tried to hand it back. With the same serious look on his face, the kid said, "No, the real one."

"Oh, go ahead, don't be such a klunk," Lisa said merrily.

"Ow ryte, myte. Y'got me," Jamie said in his awful Cockney accent, "But don't go grassin' on me to innybody else, ryte? Or I'll tell 'em I seen you buggerin' a goat."

With that, Jamie signed "Keith Moon" across the page and dotted the "I" with a little crescent moon. As the kid took the program and pen back, he didn't smile, but his eyes got huge.

"Thank you. Thank you so much. Thank you."

Jamie had the awful thought that the kid was going to kneel down and kiss his feet. Instead, the boy turned and made his way back down the row the way he had come.

"So I'm a klunk, am I?"

"No, you're a hero," Lisa flung an arm around Jamie's neck and kissed him noisily on the cheek, "You've made a fun day at the Festival into one of the high points of that kid's life. He'll buy every record the Who has ever made, decide to learn to play the drums, and drive his parents insane with his constant practicing. They'll probably shoot him and then hang themselves. And all because you were nice enough to lie to him."

Not only had their friends heard the whole thing, but the people in the rows behind and in front of them had heard as well and everyone had a good laugh at the blushing Jamie's expense.

Jamie leaned back, resting his head against the seat, and looked up. He was amazed to see how many different colors of blue actually made up the blue of the sky. At first he could not see any edges of color, just one shade drifting into the next. After a while edges presented themselves then grew into constantly shifting three dimensional shapes that slid together, then disappeared.

This is pretty good acid, and smooth as a baby's butt.

"Excuse me, Mr. Moon... "

It was a vaguely familiar voice, but Jamie was lost in the vastness of the sky and chose to ignore it. Then Lisa's elbow dug into his ribs and he pushed his head up and refocused. It was the Kid again, this time he held a piece of cardboard torn from a popcorn box.

"One more signature? Please? This one's for my Mom. Her name is Martha."

Still a little dazed, Jamie took the proffered cardboard and felt tip pen, thought a moment, then wrote, "To Martha, I'll never forget your pistol-grip ears. Keith Moon."

Holding the cardboard to his chest, the Kid began churning his way back down the row.

"Pistol-grip ears?" Lisa gave him a dubious look, "that was mean-spirited."

"Hopefully, his mother will read that, slap the shit out of him, and forbid him to come and bother me anymore."

"This should be far out," McNulty said, gesturing at the stage, "This is Zephyr, a local band from Boulder. Their guitarist is a kid named Tommy Bolin. He does a lot of edgy shit with feedback loops and stuff."

"You've seen them before?"

"Nah, just heard about 'em."

The band, a couple of them carrying guitars, were walking across the grass to the stage.

"See that big woman with the bare feet?" McNulty said, " That's Candy Givens, the lead singer. Evidently she's a trip herself."

"Holy shit!" Krenovich said as he pointed off to his right at the seats behind the end zone, "It's a piggie convention."

Jamie, following Krenovich's gesture, watched thirty or forty policemen enter the stadium and take up seats in the end zone. They wore helmets and carried clear plastic shields.

"It must be because of those crazies we heard about on the car radio." Krenovich added, "I think I can hear 'em shouting down there. Don't know if it's real or just the acid."

Jamie thought he heard some faint chanting, but with the band tuning up and doing mike checks, he wasn't sure.

"What crazies?" Jamie asked Waltz.

"I guess some people thought that the music should be free. That they shouldn't have to pay for tickets, and if enough of them came down here, they'd find a way to get in."

Then the band was announced, the drummer whacked his sticks together, and a tidal wave of rock 'n' roll hit Jamie's ears, heart, and guts. Every sense in his body opened to the music. Not just hear, feel, and see it, he could smell and taste it. Candy Givens was everything McNulty had said she'd be and more. She prowled the stage like a lioness and when she sang that she was a "Hard-Chargin' Woman" every one of the 20,000 people there believed it.

Then, too soon, the song was over and the audience roared its approval. As the crowd quieted down for the next song, down at the end of the field a different crowd noise was getting louder. There was an angry edge to it that Jamie knew didn't have much at all to do with the music. Then he saw the cops all stand up and trot out of the stands toward the out-of-sight corner of the field that was the source of the noise.

"Hey, Denver!" Candy Givens shouted over the mike, "Just ignore that shit! We came here to rock, okay?"

When half the people in her audience were craning their necks to see what was going on way off to their right and not looking at her, Givens must have immediately understood that it was her job to get their attention back.

"So if you Motherfuckers came here to rock, lemme hear you say "Yeah"!

"Yeah!" came the response.

"I said Yeah!"

"Yeah!"

"I said.... yeaheeyeaheeyeaheeee..." and the last drawn-out, growling, wailing syllable turned into a mighty fist-pumping "YEAH!"

And the band took off into a fast boogie that featured the astonishingly quick-fingered Tommy Bolin. Cops and riots forgotten, the crowd roared. At one point, the band quieted down to a steady, background rhythm while the little guitarist with the big hat was wringing sounds out of his instrument that Jamie had never heard before. Then Bolin grabbed a handle on a machine on top of his amp and pumped it around in circles. It was some kind of an adjustable echo device and the faster it was spun, the quicker was the echo. It started with a low range melodic line, then Bolin played a mid-range contrapuntal melody to his own recording. When he cranked the machine up and then played a wailing solo, people in the crowd began to stand and jump up and down, one more crank of the handle and it was a wall of sound that only ended as the performer leapt into the air. As he landed the band kicked back into the fast boogie once again and Givens sang over the cheers of the crowd.

Just as the song ended and Jamie was on his feet yelling his approval, he felt Lisa's hand on his shoulder and looked to his right where she was pointing. A billowing white cloud drifted up from beyond the end of the stands. The breeze caught it and it seemed to dissipate as it crossed the empty seats behind the end zone.

"Shit, man," Jamie said, "It looks like tear gas. Thank God it seems to be blowing the other way."

"I don't know, Babe," Lisa said, "This stadium is a like a huge bowl with openings at one end. If it catches the wind right, it can blow around in a big circle."

Jamie looked up in the sky and yelled, "Don't listen to her, God. She's just kidding. Don't do that shit, okay?"

But within a few minutes he could hear screams, coughing and choking off to his left and the agonized sounds were quickly approaching. One moment he felt okay and the next he felt like he was breathing broken glass and razor blades. His eyes stung horribly and waterfalls of tears washed down his cheeks. It was all he could do to sit in his seat and gasp for breath.

"Be cool, be cool, people," Givens rasped into the microphone, "We're getting it just as bad up here."

Jamie looked up through his tears and saw that hundreds of people had jumped over the barriers and, in an effort to get away from the gas, were streaming onto the field.

Then a man walked onto the stage with headphones around his neck, a handkerchief in one hand, and a microphone in the other. When he spoke, Jamie recognized the voice that had introduced the bands.

"She's right, folks. Just be cool. It'll pass. In the meantime, if you've got a handkerchief put it over your mouth and nose, or pull your shirt up and breath through it. And put your head down between your legs."

Lisa had a neck scarf that she put over her face, Jamie pulled up his T-shirt, and both put their heads down.

"If you people can stay cool and wait for this to pass," Givens said, then hawked, spat, and wiped her eyes, "we can damn well play for you."

And the band started into a blues lament called, appropriately enough, *Now I'm Cryin'*.

Jamie, looking through stinging eyes at the concrete between his feet, realized that the tear gas hadn't affected the acid much at all. He was still stoned to the gills and he was watching the most amazing colored patterns come up and slowly unfurl themselves out of the gray of the cement.

Then Jamie heard a pained, choking sound close by that almost sounded like a human voice. Then it came again, a little more distinctly, and it said, "Excuse me sir".

Jamie, unbelieving, looked up to see the mottled, tear-stained face of the Kid.

"Would you sign this for me?"

The Kid had a short coughing fit, then held out a red balloon.

"What the fuck..."

"It's for my Sister," he croaked.

Jamie wanted to know where the hell the kid had found a balloon and what the fuck he was going to do with it, but being unable to speak without pain, Jamie signed "Keith Moon" and the kid, sniffing and hacking, struggled his way back toward his seat.

Jamie pulled his T-shirt over his nose and went back to the patterns on the concrete.

By the time Zephyr's set was over, the effects of the tear gas were only a painful memory. The band played a rousing encore, waved to the crowd, and left the stage. Ten minutes later the members of Poco were making that long walk across the grass to the stage.

Jamie had heard their music, usually coming from Harvey's stereo, liked it, and had been glad he'd bought tickets for the night they were playing. Having grown up in the middle of the Farm Belt, everywhere he went good old-fashioned country music was blaring from every radio. Although he didn't care for overly sentimental lyrics drawled out by nasal, yodeling voices, the music had been, like it or not, the soundtrack of his boyhood. What a treat it was to hear those old country music tropes - songs about love and loss - now wrapped up in rock 'n' roll sensibilities, delivered by voices in tight harmonies, and backed by a hot pedal steel guitar.

Poco delivered a fun, upbeat, rollicking set that was a perfect change of pace from the animal power rock of Zephyr. And it set the audience up nicely for the raging, almost painful blues of the following act - Johnny Winter.

Winter first came out on stage by himself, playing an acoustic National Steel guitar and singing a throaty, heartfelt blues that made you think you were with him on a Mississippi back porch passing a bottle of whiskey between songs. Then he picked up an electric guitar and brought more of his band on stage. He was dressed all in black with a flat, wide-brimmed, black hat. His albino hair flew in long white waves as the band ripped their way through the blues like a hungry wolf in a henhouse. Then he introduced his brother Edgar, who played keyboards and sang with equal talent and power.

The acid banging around in Jamie's skull grabbed hold of some passing thought and carried Jamie away on a flood of what seemed to him to be wildly creative insight. He came back to himself eager to share this brilliance and unable to remember a shred of it. Although he was sure that he'd tripped out for only a minute or two, the sky was dark, Johnny Winter was long gone, and roadies were carrying cords and equipment around the stage.

The next act was the one that Lisa had been eagerly waiting to see - Tim Buckley.

Lisa owned both of Buckley's albums, *Goodbye and Hello* and *Happy Sad*. Every time Jamie called her it seemed that one or the other was playing in the background. So when Jamie asked her to go to the Festival and mentioned Buckley being on the Saturday night bill, Lisa started squealing. While trying to hug him and jump up and down at the same time, she banged her shoulder up under his chin which snapped his head back and almost knocked him unconscious. After a couple of woozy stumbles, she guided him down on the couch, snuggled up to him, and proceeded to make the whole thing worthwhile - the cost of the tickets, the crack on the jaw, even the missing of Hendrix on Sunday Night.

After frequent LSD trips over the past few months, Jamie had come to expect certain stages in the experience. One such was what he and his friends called "coming down off the peak". The rocket that lifted you into the stratosphere slowly turns and begins its long, slow fall back down the well of gravity. Some acid trips are unkind at these moments - your thoughts get sullen and self-critical, your body starts to ache and itch, and your tongue clacks around in the back of your mouth. You are still plenty high, but not entirely comfortable with it. But, for Jamie, this trip was different. It was like a soft, pink cloud had come up under him and, supporting his weight, let him take a slow, mellow flight homeward. He didn't know if it was due to Buckley's music or the acid. More likely a combination of both.

At the end of Buckley's set, Jamie stood up and applauded wildly. Usually when he did so it was to show an appreciation for the talent displayed. This time it was out of gratitude for a warm and emotional experience. When Buckley left the stage and the applause died down, Lisa and Jamie looked at each other, smiled, and slipped their arms around each other.

The last set of the evening was the headliner - Creedence Clear-water Revival. On the way home that night, Jamie replayed the various bands in his head. But he didn't remember that much about Creedence. They sounded exactly like their records and maybe that was the trouble. Also, when Jamie was ripped, he was very sensitive to inauthenticity and hype. So when John Fogerty got on the mic and said, in a deep Southern accent, "We want to thank y'all for comin' on out here to see us," it rankled. Mainly because Jamie knew damned well the whole band was from California.

But there was one very cool moment. About halfway through the set, a fat, gibbous moon floated up in the sky over the rim of Mile High Stadium. Fogerty saw the Moon and laughed, "We already played this one, but I think we'd better play 'er again." And for the second time that night, Creedence Clearwater Revival played *Bad Moon Rising*.

JAMIE AND THE DANCER

Jamie wasn't sure if the back seat of Ricky's Studebaker Wagon was extra soft and springy or if the purple acid he had dropped was accentuating the feeling. But every time the car hit a dip in the road or a pothole, he would rise up slowly in the air and then after a time, would gradually settle back down again. Was he really bounding along? Jamie didn't know or care. It was an interesting feeling and like other kinds of LSD fun, it was just another part of the trip.

"So Phiz," Jamie said, "what's the name of this bar where whatsher-name - your girlfriend - is dancing?"

Phiz, riding shotgun, looked back at Jamie and grinned. "Jennifer," he said, "her name is Jennifer."

Ricky turned his head around and added, "The Candlelight Lounge."

He kept looking at Jamie which was a little unnerving as Jamie could see the car was edging over into the oncoming traffic. Just in time, Ricky looked back at the road and hauled the car back into the proper lane.

"I hear it's a rough crowd out there," Ricky looked into his rear view mirror in hopes of a reaction from Jamie, "they like to beat the crap out of hippies like you guys."

Jamie rolled his eyes and said, "And another load of horseshit from Ricky Mason and his new haircut."

Ricky patted his short conservative hair and snickered back at Jamie, "just don't make eye contact, that's all I'm sayin'. One of those corn-fed farmboys catches on that you're a dirtbag hippie loaded on LSD and suddenly a fist is heading toward your face so fast there'll be smoke comin' off the knuckles."

The mental picture made Jamie's heart thump against his ribs, but he wasn't going to give Ricky the satisfaction of knowing one of his needles had landed. Besides, Ricky had popped a tab of the same acid and was just as stoned as Jamie was.

"So how come your roommate Justin didn't come along tonight?" Jamie said.

"He's only twenty. He won't be able to get into a hard liquor joint till next Winter. Anyway, I think he's going over to Angela's apartment tonight."

You just had to ask, didn't you dumbass?

* * *

Jamie had heard the song Inna-Gadda-Da-Vida more than a few times before and had thought it was a decent effort if not a particular favorite. But watching Jennifer dance to it, ripped on acid as he was, had brought his appreciation of the song up to a whole new level.

Earlier, feeling like every person they passed was secretly staring at him, Jamie had followed Phiz and Ricky through the lobby of The Weary Traveler Motel and into the Candlelight Lounge, the attached bar.

The first thing he noticed on entering was The Stones' *Gimme Shelter* playing at high volume and a tall, leggy brunette dancing on a small corner stage. Jamie would have preferred to sit in a remote, dark corner, but Phiz led them to a table in the center of the room only one table away from the stage. He had to will himself to not look at Jennifer dance while he sat down and ordered a beer from the waitress. Only then could he let what she was doing possess his whole focus. It was as if her body was shouting with its own voice, as if it was saying, "pay attention, this is important!"

When the song ended, Jamie slapped his hands together, loudly at first, then more quietly as he noticed people were turning to look at him. The stage lights dimmed and Jennifer threw a diaphanous wrap around her skimpy costume and came over to the table. She was every inch the beautiful girl in Phiz's picture with the Nefertiti eye makeup and false eyelashes so long and thick Jamie felt she could swat flies with them. As she snuggled up to Phiz, he introduced her to Ricky and Jamie and told her that all three of them were high on LSD.

"That is so cool," she said, "I sometimes wish there was a club that only acidheads could get into. I'd dance there every night if I could. You guys can get things the regular bar crowd doesn't even see. I've got a special treat lined up for my next set, you're going to love it."

As she said this she reached out, squeezed Jamie's hand and gave him a shy smile so full of promise that it nearly made his eyes go blurry. During the rest of the break she talked about studying Wicca, the oldest of all the religions.

"Is that some kind of Devil worship?" Ricky asked.

"No, no, no," was the answer. "There is no such thing as the Devil. He was made up to scare people into letting themselves be controlled by the priests. Wicca says that there are many natural forces, both positive and negative, and you must respect them all. Some will help you and there are others that will make your life miserable if you don't give them their proper due."

Her statements didn't make a whole lot of sense to Jamie, but at least it made more sense to him than most organized religions did.

Jamie was fascinated by Jennifer. She was, in most ways, not like anything he'd been expecting. Instead of a bored, shuffle-around-to-the-music go-go dancer, she was a talented, interpretive artist. Instead of someone who was brittle, cold, and as soft as a sidewalk, she was a kind and gentle soul. And instead of being vapid and shallow, she liked to discuss ideas. Way out there ideas, sure, but ideas nonetheless.

Jennifer glanced at the clock, said she had to go prepare for her next set, and went over to talk to the bartender.

"I think she's going to do Inna-Gadda-Da-Vida now," Phiz said, "It should be fun. Almost every time she does it, there's some loudmouth who starts making rude remarks. If they do, near the end of the song she'll throw a curse at them."

Jamie and Ricky looked at each other, then back at Phiz, and simultaneously said, "What?"

"Like this," Phiz held out his hand. He'd folded the two middle fingers of his hand down to his palm and he was holding the thumb and the index and pinkie finger out straight.

"At UT in Austin that's the 'Hook-em-Horns' sign," Ricky said.

"Yeah, I suppose, but down there they also think that I've Been Workin' on the Railroad is really The Eyes of Texas are Upon You. Just watch for it, that's all I'm saying."

So here she was, dancing the outlines of the Garden of Eden story while Jamie watched, spellbound. Part of the "special treat" for acidheads was she had painted her fingernails with black light responsive paint and had had the bartender turn on a UV light bulb over the stage. As she moved, her fingernails left glowing bright blue trails in the air. She didn't try to portray characters, instead she danced the emotions they were feeling - innocence, discovery, attraction, love, and lust. Then, as the entrance of the Serpent gave way to wild and frenetic motion, evil and power seduced the characters.

Right behind Jamie, and almost on cue, a table full of frat boys from the College started yelling out rude comments. Jennifer's eyes seemed to flash with anger and Jamie was so tightly tied into the performance he could feel her reaching down inside to transmute that fury into power.

"Take it off!" yelled one of the frat boys and two others added, "Yeah, baby!"

Jennifer turned around and stooped over an imaginary fire in the center of the stage and seemed to pluck a hot coal out of the flames. Just as the lead guitar began to screech in agony, she spun around and her hand, set in the demonic curse, came up and over her shoulder and straight out at the table behind Jamie. Although there was nothing visible in the air, it felt to Jamie like someone had shot a flamethrower over his shoulder.

Jamie jerked around in his seat expecting to see three smoldering corpses and instead saw the three totally oblivious frat boys giggling and swilling beer.

The next thing Jamie knew he was once again in the back seat of the Studebaker and they seemed to be heading back into town.

"Uhh.." Jamie started, then cleared his throat to try again, "Where are we going?"

Ricky looked up into the rear view mirror as his eyebrows shot up. "Oh my God," he gasped theatrically, "It talks!"

Phiz turned in his seat and looked back at Jamie, shaking his head. "Dude," he said, "Where have you been? We watched Jennifer dance until the end of her set, then Ricky wanted to leave and you were in some parallel zombie universe, so I said goodbye to Jennifer and we split."

"Sorry. That Inna-Gadda-Da-Vida trip freaked me out, I guess. But I'm cool now. We goin' back to Fifth Street?"

"Oh yeah," said Ricky, "there must be six or eight psychedelicized hippies floatin' around in there and Lyle, who found some crank to shoot up, talkin' their legs off. Should be hysterical."

* * *

The house was pretty much as Ricky had predicted it would be. Lyle was in one corner chain-smoking and talking a blue streak about businessmen riding on the backs of the common grunt soldier, Shoes tossing in conspiracy theories about Nixon and Agnew plotting to rescind the Bill of Rights, and McNulty chuckling as he watched the giant caterpillar of a mustache on Lyle's upper lip wriggling wildly.

Jamie, making his way through the house, came upon Jason who was holding something up over his right shoulder. With a casual flip, he threw it straight down at the floor. It stopped then snapped back up into Jason's hand.

"Wow!" Jamie said, "A yo-yo. Where'd you get that?"

"My parent's house. They keep a lot of my old shit in boxes down in the basement."

Jason threw the yo-yo down again, let it hover just above the floor, then twitched the string and it zipped back up into his hand.

"Actually I found three. Krenovich has got one, and Waltz has another."

I glanced toward the kitchen and could see one yo-yo fly straight out and back again and another describe a big circle before it returned.

"Ha! tricky shit, man," Jamie said, "maybe I'll get a turn later. Right now I got some bad cottonmouth. Later, Dude."

Once in the kitchen, Jamie opened the fridge to find a plastic pitcher of pink liquid and very little else.

Fuckin' Zasko, Jamie thought as he put the pitcher next to the sink and began rummaging the cupboards for a clean glass. When Jamie was still working at the Hargreaves/Johnson cafeteria he lifted a quart-sized can of Zasko Powdered Drink Mix and took it home. Two scoops of powder mixed with a pitcher of water made a quart of really crappy fake Kool-Aid.

So whattya want for nothin'?

Jamie found a juice glass, poured it half full, and knocked it back.

As he put the pitcher back, he noticed something very odd going on with his jaw muscles. They were flexing involuntarily about once a second. Then the muscle group that opened his jaws started flexing alternately causing his mouth to open and then close, rhythmically, making his teeth click together. He tried to keep his jaw closed but failed and the click - click - click of his teeth slamming together went on.

For a little while, Jamie thought this was just a harmless part of the trip and tried to focus on something else, but instead of settling down, the involuntary snapping of his jaws grew more insistent and powerful. Worried about possibly breaking some teeth, he tried putting a couple of knuckles in his mouth. The bites quickly became painful.

Jamie rushed to a cupboard where he remembered he'd seen half a box of stale saltine crackers, fumbled open a packet and started stuffing crackers in his mouth. His jaw kept up its insistent slamming, but at least his teeth were being protected by the crushed crackers.

Then his tongue joined in, shoving the cracker crumbs around in his mouth, then pulling back just in time to avoid being caught between the relentlessly slamming teeth.

Holy Shit, Jamie thought, *it's like something has taken over my mouth.*

And fear started to creep into Jamie's head.

What if it doesn't stop? Jamie thought as he shoved a couple more crackers into his out-of-control mouth, *what's it going to take over next?*

As if in answer to his question, his tongue and throat muscles all rolled together in such a big swallow-motion it snapped his head back. Again and again Jamie swallowed in huge waves that started in his mouth and traveled halfway down his esophagus. He had to hold onto the edge of the counter just to keep his feet.

With only a small amount of relief, he noticed that his jaws and teeth had settled down and were no longer dangerously slamming together. What worried him now was that the relentless, huge swallowing motions were generating peristaltic waves that travelled down through his chest and into his stomach.

That was when Jamie realized what had happened to him. He'd been cursed.

Jennifer had said, "you guys can get things the regular bar crowd doesn't even see." Well, he'd got something all right. Although he knew it was not intended for him, something must have been riding on that curse she threw, jumped off and wormed its way into his acid-soaked, impressionable mind. Like a kid with a new toy, this entity was now trying out the controls to his whole digestive tract.

As his stomach began to roil and squirm, Jamie wiped the crumbs, spit, and tears off his pallid face with a damp washcloth, then went looking for Phiz.

"Phiz!" Jamie cried as the tall man stepped out of the bathroom, zipping up his pants.

"Hey, Jamie," Phiz said, "What's up, bro? You're lookin' kinda freaked out."

"Yeah, no shit. You remember that curse that Jennifer threw back at the Whatchamacallit Lounge? I think I got some of it."

Phiz's eyebrows shot up.

"What do you mean?"

"Something has, like, taken over in parts of my body. Like chewing motions so big I thought they were going to break my teeth, and then giant and repeated swallowing movements. Now my guts are just writhing."

"Bummer, Dude. What can I do to help?"

"Do you think Jennifer might know how to stop it or turn it around?"

""I doubt it, man. But it'd be worth an ask. She just got off a little while ago and should be home by now."

A few minutes later, they were on their way out to Jamie's car. Jamie had to stop for a moment and hold onto a tree for support. The exaggerated, involuntary moments had descended to the lower part of his abdomen.

"Ouch, God dammit!" Jamie grimaced.

It felt as if a section of his gut was being way overinflated, then that pain would subside only to be replaced by a similar pain in another area.

"You mind driving?" Jamie asked as he handed over the keys, "I'm a little too fucked up."

They reached the car and just as he grasped the door handle, Jamie farted. Not a squeaker, or a silent-but-deadly, or a little fizz-fazz, this was a rolling thunder of an Elephant Fart. In deep and sonorous tones it rumbled on for a long time. When it was over, Jamie nearly fell to his knees in relief.

Phiz tried to choke off a laugh, failed, and guffawed loudly.

"Sorry man," Phiz chortled, "But that was the loudest, most king-sized fart I've ever heard."

"No offense taken. You know what?" Jamie said as he straightened up, "I think it's gone. The curse, I mean. It ran all through me and then blew itself out."

"You feel okay now?"

"Yeah, I feel great. Jesus, that was weird," Jamie said, "if you want to go see Jennifer, you can borrow my car. I think I'll go back in the house and see if I can cop a turn on one of those yo-yos."

Jamie headed for the house, then stopped and yelled back, "Oh and tell Jennifer to be careful who she points that thing at, okay"

Phiz just laughed and waved as he climbed into the car. Jamie turned back to the house.